Rudolph the Red Nosed Horse?

By Emily Claire Rowland

Illustrated by: J. Z. Sagario
Colored by: Roy Ugang

To order additional copies of this book, contact:
Xlibris Corporation
1-888-795-4274
www.Xlibris.com
Orders@Xlibris.com

It was a farm like any other farm; there were beautiful meadows where sheep pounced around, a pond for the ducks, a barn and pasture for horses, fields for cows and goats, and a regular country farm house. This was a morning, like every other morning too; the farmer would come out to milk the cows, gather eggs from the chickens, and feed the goats, cows, horses and sheep.

All of the animals on the farm had a job, the cows and goats gave milk, the chickens lay the eggs, and the horses pull the plow. But one young horse in the barn didn't want to pull the plow. In a stall was Rudolph, a bay, about three years old. Each morning when the sun came up, and every night when the moon rose, Rudolph was looking outside to the hills in the north. Something always made him look in that direction.

The farmer would come in, take him out to the meadow for a run before putting him to work on the plow. Rudolph liked being hitched up, but going back and forth in the same fields every day was pretty boring...he knew there was something more.

One magical night, Rudolph was looking out his window towards the north. He heard a sound, a jingle of sorts; he blinked his eyes a few times, because he thought he might be dreaming. Over the trees heading right towards the farm were some flying horses pulling a wagon! He shook his head, because he couldn't believe what he was seeing. Wait, those weren't horses, they were deer...and there was a chubby man in a red suit in the wagon they pulled. He could hear the man saying "Ho...Ho...Ho!" The deer brought the wagon down on top of the farm house and the man got out and disappeared into the chimney!

Rudolph still couldn't believe his eyes. He called out to the deer, "Who are you?" The deer in the front smiled and replied, "Why we are Santa's reindeer. This is Christmas Eve and we are helping Santa bring gifts to all the children of the world."

"Wow", Rudolph thought, that must be exciting, to fly all over the world. "How do you become Santa's reindeer?" he asked. The deer replied, "You must be from the North Pole. Santa chooses us when he sees us fly." Rudolph was curious, "But how do you learn to fly?" "Well," the reindeer said, "first you must be a reindeer."

Santa came out of the chimney, climbed into the wagon and they were gone as quickly as they came. Rudolph didn't sleep much that night, but when he did, he dreamed about flying. When he awoke, the sun was up; he saw birds flying around and sighed. "They must be training to be Santa's reindeer." Then he had an idea. What if he learned how to fly, he knew how to pull the plow, pulling Santa's wagon wouldn't be hard, just figuring out how to fly, and that would be the trick.

Rudolph went to Skiddles, his very best friend the cow and told her what he saw the night before. He told her how he wanted to become one of Santa's reindeer. "How can you do that?" she asked. "You're a horse, not a deer." She thought for a while. "Wait, there are some very friendly deer in the woods, maybe they can teach you."

Rudolph couldn't wait to get to the meadow the next morning. Skiddles followed him and introduced him to the deer. He told them what he wanted to do and they agreed to help. "We don't know how to fly, but we can make you look like a deer" they said. First they got sticks and dipped them in tree sap and stuck them on his head. "Hmmm," said Buddy, one of the deer, "that works for antlers, but you have a mane and a long tail that we don't have." Skiddles had an idea; she called Billy, her friend the goat and whispered something into his ear. Billy raised an eyebrow when looking at Rudolph and then quickly pounced on him.

The next thing Rudolph knew, his tail and mane were trimmed.

Well, now he looked like a reindeer, but how could he fly? Just then Trixie, a funny little woodpecker landed in the tree above him and started pecking on the wood. Rudolph looked up. He called to her and asked "Can you teach me how to fly?" Trixie looked at Rudolph turning her head to the side, "Do what???!!!" she asked. "Teach me how to fly so that I can help Santa deliver gifts to all the children of the world." he proudly replied. Trixie shrugged her shoulders, "Sure, why not."

Trixie flew down onto Rudolph's back and looked around. "How can I teach you to fly if you don't have wings?" she asked. "Santa's deer just ran and jumped into the air and flew" he replied. Rudolph ran and jumped into the air and came down with a thud! He tried again, and again, and again. Tired, he dropped down to take a rest under a large redwood. A voice from high in the tree said, "You knooooowwwww you can't fly, whoo hooo." Rudolph looked up. There in the tree branches was a large old owl. Trixie flew up and said "If Santa's deer can fly, why can't Rudolph?" The owl went on to say "They have walked thruuuuuu the Northern Lights to get their magic. Rudolph must walk thruuuuuu the lights to get his magic toooo whooo whoooo."

"How do I get to the Northern Lights?" asked Rudolph. "Youuuuuu must travel to the far noooorrrrth." said the owl. "Walk thruuuuuu the lights and keep going north until you reach the Nooorrrth Pole" he said.

The next day Rudolph, Skiddles, and Trixie set out for their long journey north. Rudolph was determined to follow his dream.

When they reached the northern lights, they all stopped in their tracks. This was the most beautiful site they had ever seen. Every color of the rainbow painted across the sky. Rudolph took a deep breath and stepped through the lights. The lights made him feel as light as air. Skiddles and Trixie followed.

Once they were all on the other side of the lights, Rudolph tried to fly again. This time he didn't land with a thud. He floated for a bit before landing lightly on his hooves. Trixie and Skiddles were wide eyed with excitement. "You flew, you flew!" they said. Rudolph knew he was getting closer to making his dream come true.

The three friends continued their trip north, through trees and snow until they saw a village filled with small people. Rudolph saw the reindeer that talked to him at the farm. "This must be the North Pole" he said. Rudolph ran down the hill to the village as fast as he could, almost falling over with excitement. "I'm here, I'm here" he called to the reindeer. The reindeer looked up, surprised to see a horse running towards him with stick antlers stuck to his head.

"You have come a long way" the reindeers said. "Yes", said Rudolph "and I am here to learn how to fly so I can help Santa." As he said this, Santa came walking up. "Blitzen has told me all about you Rudolph". Santa said. "I have never had a flying horse pull my sleigh." Rudolph looked sad. "But there is a first time for everything" Santa said, patting Rudolph on the back. "Blitzen, teach this horse how to fly!"

Rudolph worked very hard and the next thing you knew, he was flying just as good as all of the reindeer. That Christmas Eve, Santa came to Rudolph and asked him. "Rudolph with your spirit so bright, won't you guide my sleigh tonight?" Rudolph was the happiest horse in the world. He got hitched to Santa's sleigh and away they went, taking gifts to all the children of the world.

Skiddles and Trixie watched as they flew away, so happy their friend had followed his dream. Skiddles looking up at the moon asked. "Do you think the Northern Lights gave me magic to fly too?" Trixie smiled "Maybe so!" Skiddles looking fondly towards the sky replied "I've always wanted to go over the moon".

Could Skiddles fly? Could she jump over the moon? Well that is another story.